THE NATURE GIRLS

Aki

To my sisters, Evelyne and Annie

Laura

Miffy

Annie

Rebecca

Jane

Vanessa

June

Melanie

MEET THE
NATURE
GIRLS

Sarah

Cathleen

Lucy

Zoe

Kirsten

Tilly

Joy

Emily

We're Nature Girls! We must explore.
We pack our bags, we're out the door . . .

. . . and off we go! There's much to see.
We'll start our journey by the sea.

A pod of **dolphins**
swims nearby.
The fish come, too.
We all say, "Hi!"

It's time to go.
We march along.
We smile at birds
and share their song.

On we trek, across the land.
Up ahead, we see some sand!

A camel pads up to our side.
He takes us for a bumpy ride.

In tall grass, we creep up slow.
All around are buffalo.

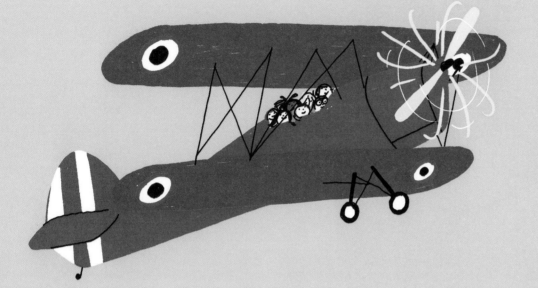

See ya, plains! It's been nice!
Now we're off to find some ice!

A tawny owl! She sees us, too.
She hoots a question, "Whooo are you?"

The tundra has snow everywhere.
Look, how cute – an Arctic hare!

There's one more stop on our big trip.
We've got our compass and our ship!

The forest is
lush and filled
with sound.
Look at all this
life we've found!

It's hard to leave, but we must go.
There's more to see
                    and do
                         and know.

MEET THE BIOMES

A **biome** is a community of plants and animals that covers a large area of the earth. Temperature, soil and the amount of light and water help determine the kinds of plants and animals that can live in that area.

Aquatic

Salt water or fresh water, there are so many plants and creatures that live below the surface. Water covers nearly three quarters of the earth – there's a lot to explore!

Desert

Deserts are dry. There isn't much rain – around 250mm a year. In many deserts, days are very hot, and nights are very cold.

Grassland

Grasslands are covered with grasses! There aren't many trees. It rains more than in a desert, but less than in a forest. Many animals are grazers – grass-eaters!

Tundra

The tundra is the coldest. No trees live here. There is a thick layer of frozen ground called permafrost. Not many animals live here all year round.

Forest

Forests are full of trees and other woody plants. They get more rain than other biomes. Lots of different kinds of animals live here.

First published in the USA 2019 by Henry Holt and Company
First published in the UK 2019 by Macmillan Children's Books
an imprint of Pan Macmillan
20 New Wharf Road, London N1 9RR
Associated companies throughout the world
www.panmacmillan.com

ISBN (PB): 978-1-5290-0484-7